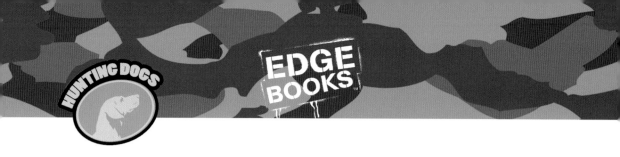

POINTERS

LOYAL HUNTING COMPANIONS

BY TAMMY GAGNE

CONSULTANT:
ROBERT RETTICK
MEMBER
AMERICAN HUNTING DOG CLUB

CAPSTONE PRESS
a capstone imprint

Edge Books are published by Capstone Press,
1710 Roe Crest Drive, North Mankato, Minnesota 56003
www.capstonepub.com

Library of Congress Cataloging-in-Publication Data
Gagne, Tammy.
  Pointers : loyal hunting companions / by Tammy Gagne.
      p. cm. — (Edge books. hunting dogs)
  Includes bibliographical references and index.
  Summary: "Describes the history, care, and training of pointers used for hunting"—
Provided by publisher.
  ISBN 978-1-4296-9908-2 (library binding)
  ISBN 978-1-62065-935-9 (paper over board)
  ISBN 978-1-4765-1547-2 (eBook PDF)
  1. Pointer (Dog breed)—Juvenile literature. I. Title.
  SF429.P7G34 2013
  636.75—dc23   2012027110

Editorial Credits
Angie Kaelberer, editor; Kyle Grenz, designer; Marcie Spence, media researcher;
Jennifer Walker, production specialist

Photo Credits
Alamy Images: Juniors Bildarchiv GmbH, 10; Dreamstime: Mphoto2, 25 (bottom
left); Capstone Studio: Karon Dubke, 25 (top left); Fiona Green, 27; Fotolia: Dogs,
21; iStockphotos: JMichl, 4, LUGO, 24 (top), Visual Communications, 28 (top);
Shutterstock: Africa Studio, 25 (top right), AnetaPics, 7 (top), Arman Zhenikeyev, 19
(bottom), auremar, 29, Barna Tanko, 16 (top), 17 (bottom), 26 (bottom), bitt24, cover
(back), Brian Goodman 26 (top), Brian Guest, 5, Burry van den Brick, 8, Elnur, 25
(middle left), F.C.G., 19 (top), 22, 23, 24 (bottom), Jack Cronkhite, 14, Kaleb Madsen,
cover (front), 9, Lee319, 6, Lenkadan, 16 (bottom), Liga Gabrane, 15, Linn Currie,
1, 13, Marsan, 12, Nick Hayes, 28 (bottom), Petra Vavrova, 11, Svetlana Valoueva,
17 (top), thelefty, 20, Vitaly Titov & Maria Sidelnikova, 25 (bottom right), Zuzule, 7
(bottom), 18

Printed in the United States of America in Stevens Point, Wisconsin.
092012   006937WZS13

TABLE OF CONTENTS

CHAPTER 1

POINTING THE WAY

When you brought your pointer puppy home, you wondered if she would ever grow into her tail. Now your hunting partner has found a bird in the field. She's an amazing sight with her tail out straight, right front leg held up, and nose pointed forward. She's shown you where the game is. Now she stands perfectly still, waiting for your next command.

Pointers show hunters the location of game.

POINTER HISTORY

Pointers are one of the oldest hunting dogs. They are shown in paintings from the 1500s. The first pointers were from Spain and Portugal. By about 1650 the breed had made its way to England.

In England pointers were crossbred with several other dog breeds. Today's pointers include foxhounds, bloodhounds, greyhounds, and various types of setters in their ancestry.

The Vizsla pointer breed began in the 1100s.

5

AMERICAN POINTERS

English pointers were introduced to the United States in the late 1800s. A famous pointer called Sensation arrived in 1876. You may have seen Sensation without even knowing it. His picture has been featured on the Westminster Kennel Club's logo for more than 100 years. Each year Westminster hosts one of the world's most famous dog shows.

At first, hunters in the United States weren't interested in the English pointer. They preferred to hunt with setter breeds. Pointers weren't even allowed to take part in **field trials** with setters. But around 1910, the rules changed. When pointers were allowed to compete in trials, they began winning. Pointers then became popular with American hunters.

The English pointer is now known just as the pointer.

field trial—a competition at which dogs demonstrate hunting skills

6

Pointers are still among the top dogs at field trials. Other pointing breeds include the Brittany, the German shorthaired and wirehaired pointers, the Weimaraner, and the Vizsla. The American Kennel Club (AKC) also lists the Spinone Italiano as a pointing breed. This breed is mainly found in Europe.

Spinone Italiano

Pointing stance

POINTERS AND HUNTING

A pointing dog's job is to find and locate birds and other game. It stops and points its nose in the direction of the game. When the dog points, it will sometimes raise one of its front legs and extend its tail straight back. This is called the pointing stance. Pointers are best known for their ability to locate birds such as grouse, pheasant, and quail.

Like pointers, setters also point to game. At one time, pointers and setters pointed in slightly different ways. Setters crouched down, or set, when they pointed. Hunters trained them to do this so they could throw a net over the game without catching the dog in it. By the late 1700s, most hunters used guns instead of nets. Guns made it unnecessary to train setters to lower their bodies in this way.

Today the biggest difference between pointers and setters is the length of their hair. Pointers have much shorter coats than setters. Many owners see a pointer's shorter coat as an advantage. It needs much less grooming and also keeps a dog cooler in the field.

German shorthaired pointer

CHAPTER 2

PICKING A POINTER

Pointers are among the best canine athletes. It is no accident that these dogs are members of the American Kennel Club (AKC) sporting group. Their speed and **birdiness** are the main reasons why so many hunters choose these dogs as hunting partners. Each breed also has a unique **temperament** that can make it the best choice for you.

birdiness—natural talent for bird hunting

temperament—combination of behavior and personality

The pointer is known for being alert and even-tempered in the field. This intelligent breed is not easily distracted from its work. Some hunting breeds are divided into two separate types—field dogs used for hunting and bench dogs that compete in dog shows. But not the pointer. Pointers are still bred for the same qualities as they were 100 years ago. A pointer that wins titles in the show ring has the same look and temperament as a dog that hunts with its owner.

Weimaraner

A Noble Breed

The Weimaraner breed began in the early 1800s. Sportsmen in the court of Grand Duke Karl August in Weimar, Germany, developed the dog to hunt large game. Only royalty were allowed to breed or own what was then called the Weimar pointer. By the late 1800s, the breed name had changed to Weimaraner.

In 1938 American hunter Howard Knight persuaded the German Weimaraner Club to sell him four young Weimaraner dogs. Knight began the breed in the United States. During World War II, many German breeders sent their Weimaraners to the United States for safety.

In the 1950s U.S. President Dwight Eisenhower owned a Weimaraner named Heidi. The presidential pet sparked Americans' interest in the breed. That wasn't always a good thing. Careless breeders began producing dogs with health or temperament problems. The Weimaraner breed later recovered and is now more popular for hunting in the United States than it is in Germany.

FINDING A BREEDER

The best place to find a pointing dog is from a breeder with a good reputation. You can find the names of good pointer breeders in your area by contacting local hunting clubs, breed associations, and other pointer owners. When you visit the breeder, ask to see where the dogs are kept and to meet the puppies' parents.

Breeders can often tell which pups will grow up to be the best hunting dogs. You can also increase your odds of getting a good hunter by checking the puppy's **pedigree**. The best hunting dogs usually have hunting champions as parents or grandparents.

POINTER BREEDS

Breed	Colors	Height	Weight
Pointer	white with dark brown, yellow, black, or light red-brown markings	23 to 28 inches (58 to 71 cm)	44 to 75 pounds (20 to 34 kg)
German Shorthaired Pointer	liver or liver and white	21 to 25 inches (53 to 64 cm)	45 to 70 pounds (20 to 32 kg)
German Wirehaired Pointer	dark brown and white	22 to 26 inches (56 to 66 cm)	55 to 70 pounds (25 to 32 kg)
Brittany	light red-brown and white; dark brown and white	17 ½ to 20 ½ inches (44 to 52 cm)	30 to 40 pounds (14 to 18 kg)
Weimaraner	solid gray	23 to 27 inches (58 to 69 cm)	55 to 80 pounds (25 to 36 kg)
Wirehaired Pointing Griffon	gray and brown; white and brown; white and light red-brown	20 to 24 inches (51 to 61 cm)	35 to 70 pounds (16 to 32 kg)
Vizsla	red-brown	21 to 24 inches (53 to 61 cm)	45 to 65 pounds (20 to 29 kg)

pedigree—list of a dog's ancestors

13

POINTER BREEDS

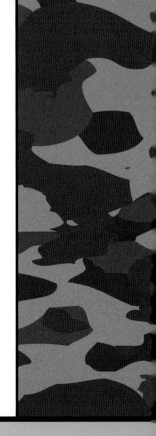

The pointer is famous for its skill at finding birds. But it is also a great family dog. These energetic dogs love to run. They do best living with an active family with a large fenced-in yard.

The German shorthaired pointer is smart and good-natured. This breed has some special hunting abilities. In addition to birds, it has a talent for pointing to deer, opossums, and raccoons. More German shorthaired pointers are **registered** with the AKC than any other pointing breed.

German shorthaired pointers hunt deer and other animals.

The German shorthaired pointer usually behaves well around other dogs. But its strong **prey drive** can make it a poor choice for homes with cats and other smaller pets.

The German wirehaired pointer shares many qualities with its smoother-coated cousin. But because of its longer hair, the German wirehaired pointer needs a bit more grooming. Its wiry coat allows it to hunt equally well on land and in the water.

register—to record a dog's breeding records with an official club

prey drive—urge to chase another animal

The Brittany's official name was once the Brittany spaniel. It looks a lot like the Welsh springer spaniel. But it performs like a pointer when hunting. For this reason the word "spaniel" was dropped from the breed's name in 1982. The Brittany finds, hunts, and retrieves all types of game birds. The breed performs well both in the field and the show ring.

The Brittany is now part of the pointer group.

The sleek gray Weimaraner once hunted wolves, deer, and even bears. Like other pointers, it's now mainly a bird dog. It also makes a good family pet.

Weimaraner

 DOG FACT

The Weimaraner is nicknamed "the gray ghost" because of its gray coat and light-colored eyes.

German wirehaired pointer

The wirehaired pointing griffon's rough coat might make it look untidy, but its fur actually protects it. The griffon doesn't seem to be bothered by underbrush that would scratch a smooth-coated dog.

Vizsla

Some pointers retrieve game as well as point. The Vizsla breed is especially known for its retrieving ability.

CHAPTER 3

CLASS IS IN SESSION

New pointer owners often have many questions. When is the best time to begin training? What is the difference between obedience training and hunter training? Should you train your dog yourself or get help from a trainer?

Start training your new pointer puppy as soon as you bring it home. Most puppies will be between 7 and 12 weeks old at that time. Begin by teaching your pointer its name and basic obedience commands such as "come" and "stay." Once your pup knows the basic commands, you can begin teaching it commands used in hunting.

18

A professional trainer can advise you on training your pointer.

You may decide to get the help of a dog training professional or attend a training class. But the trainer shouldn't train your dog for you. He or she should teach you how to train your dog.

Start by teaching your dog basic commands.

Training is about building a relationship between you and your dog. As you work together, you get to know each other and build trust. A dog is also most likely to obey the person who trains it.

TRAINING BASICS

When training your pointer, teach one command at a time. Practice until your dog knows the command well before moving on to the next one. Always use the same wording for a particular command. Reward your dog with praise when it does what you ask. Never punish your dog during training. If your pointer does something it shouldn't, tell it "no" in a firm tone of voice.

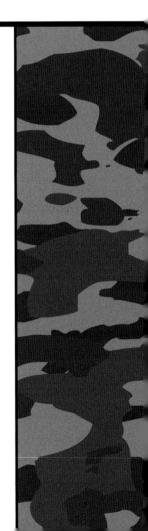

Once your pointer understands a command, practice it in different spots. Varying locations will help make sure that your dog will obey when you hunt in new places.

Other obedience commands a pointer must learn include "whoa" and "heel." When you say "whoa," your dog should stop in its tracks. A dog that follows this command is less likely to get into trouble. It also won't scare game away before you are ready to fire your weapon.

heel—a command telling a dog to walk by a person's side

POINTING TRAINING

Once your dog knows the basic commands, begin working on its pointing skills in a field or in the woods. This will help build your pointer's excitement for the sport. Be careful not to tire out your dog, though. As your pup gets bigger, it will have more energy.

Adult pointers use their sense of smell to find birds. But puppies rely on their eyesight while they are first learning to hunt. Take your pup into the woods where it will see and investigate wild birds.

You can also buy a bird from a game farm and bring it to the woods in a cage. Release the bird in front of your puppy, allowing it to see and smell the bird. Let your pointer chase the bird for a short distance, but don't allow the dog to injure or kill the bird. You can use a **check cord** to control your pup while training. If your dog starts to point, use the "whoa" command to stop it in its tracks. Then reward your dog with lots of praise.

check cord—a long cord attached to a dog's collar

Your pointer will probably chase squirrels and rabbits at this point, as well as birds. You can discourage chasing small animals with a gentle but firm "no." Over time, your pointer will come to understand that you want it to focus on birds.

Once your pointer is comfortable with sniffing out birds, you can introduce it to gunfire. Use a cap pistol or a gun with blank bullets at first. Shoot the gun when the pointer is focused on a bird. The dog will then think of the gunshot as part of something fun. If your dog acts scared, work on bird training a bit more before trying the gun again.

LEARNING TO RETRIEVE

Many pointers don't retrieve game. But if you want your pointer to retrieve, it must learn to give you the game on command. You can use a **dummy** when teaching this command. Throw the dummy away from your puppy. When your pup brings the dummy back to you, praise it and say, "give" as you gently take the dummy from its mouth.

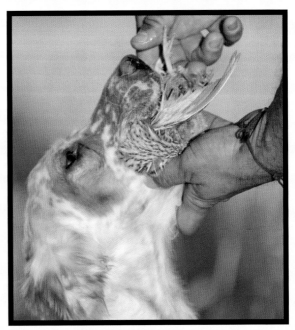

dummy—a training toy

Your pointer may return to you but then refuse to drop the dummy. If this happens, lean down and blow into your pup's ear. Praise your dog when it drops the dummy. You can let the pup smell the dummy, but don't allow it to take it back into its mouth.

TRAINING EQUIPMENT

check cord—**used to control and restrain the dog**

whistle—
**can be used
for commands**

training or cap pistol—
**used to get the dog comfortable
with the sound of gunfire**

crate—**used to get
the dog familiar with
riding in a vehicle**

bumpers or dummies—
used in retriever training

CHAPTER 4

YOUR POINTER AT HOME

Your pointer depends on you to keep it safe and healthy both in the field and at home. Take your dog to a veterinarian for a checkup at least once a year. Your vet will vaccinate your pointer against rabies and other illnesses. Also, ticks, fleas, and mosquitoes

can bite your dog and cause diseases such as heartworm. Your vet can give your pointer medications to help keep it safe from these diseases.

Your pointer needs a healthy diet. Hunting dogs need to eat more protein and fat than other dogs do. Look for a high-energy food at your local pet supply store.

Most pointer breeds have short coats that need little grooming. Brush your pointer once a week, and bathe it only when it gets very dirty. The wirehaired pointing griffon's rough coat may need to be brushed slightly more often.

Wirehaired pointing griffon

HEALTH ISSUES

Several health problems can affect pointers, including **hip dysplasia**. In many cases dogs are born with this condition, but it doesn't show up until later in life. Signs include lameness, hopping, and trouble standing up. Sometimes surgery is needed.

Another problem that can affect pointers is progressive retinal atrophy (PRA). This eye disease usually strikes dogs that are at least 2. PRA isn't painful, but it will keep your dog from hunting once it starts to lose its eyesight.

When choosing your puppy, ask the breeder for paperwork from the Orthopedic Foundation of America (OFA). Both of the pup's parents should be tested and cleared for hip dysplasia. Both parents should also be cleared by the Canine Eye Registry Foundation (CERF) for PRA. The clearances mean that your pointer should be much less likely to develop these conditions.

> hip dysplasia—a condition in which a dog's hip joints do not fit together properly

TIME FOR FUN

Pointers are known for their energy. A well-trained adult can hunt for hours without getting bored. But while hunting may be your pointer's favorite pastime, it shouldn't be its only one. Make time for your dog every day. Take your pointer for a walk, play games in the yard, or let it run around

at an enclosed dog park. What you choose to do is much less important than spending time with your dog.

Many pointers do well in agility competitions.

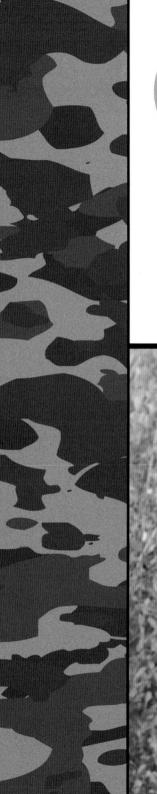

In 2005 a German shorthaired pointer named Carlee won Best in Show at the Westminster Dog Show.

Pointing breeds make excellent hunting companions. Their friendly personalities also make them great pets. If you take the time to train and care for your pointer, you'll have both a good hunting companion and a family friend.

GLOSSARY

birdiness (BURD-ee-nuhss)—a dog's natural talent for bird hunting

check cord (CHEK KORD)—a long cord attached to a dog's collar that is used to bring the dog to a sudden stop

dummy (DUHM-ee)—a training toy used as a substitute for a bird

field trial (FEELD TRYE-uhl)—a competition at which dogs demonstrate hunting skills

heel (HEEL)—a command telling a dog to walk by a person's side

hip dysplasia (HIP dis-PLAY-zhah)—a condition in which an animal's hip joints do not fit together properly

pedigree (PED-uh-gree)—a list of a dog's ancestors

prey drive (PRAY DRYVE)—the urge to chase another animal

register (REJ-uh-stur)—to record a dog's breeding records with an official club

temperament (TEM-pur-uh-muhnt)—the combination of a dog's behavior and personality

READ MORE

Gagne, Tammy. *German Shorthaired Pointer.* Breed Lover's Guide. Neptune City, N.J.: T.F.H. Publications, 2011.

Wilcox, Charlotte. *Weimaraners.* All about Dogs. Mankato, Minn.: Capstone Press, 2011.

Young, Jeff C. *Pheasant Hunting for Kids.* Into the Great Outdoors. North Mankato, Minn.: Capstone Press, 2013.

INTERNET SITES

FactHound offers a safe, fun way to find Internet sites related to this book. All of the sites on FactHound have been researched by our staff.

Here's all you do:

Visit *www.facthound.com*

Type in this code: 9781429699082

Super-cool stuff! Check out projects, games and lots more at **www.capstonekids.com**

INDEX